Marie
from Paris

Hello, I am Marie from Paris! Come inside to meet my family and my friends...

Françoise Sabatier-Morel
& Isabelle Pellegrini

Illustrated by
Princesse Camcam

FICTION READALONG
AV2 BY WEIGL™
ADDED VALUE • AUDIO VISUAL

www.av2books.com

First Published by

abc melody™

My name is Marie. I am seven years old. I live in Paris, the capital of France. Paris is a very beautiful city and home to historical monuments, huge museums, department stores, gourmet restaurants, lovely parks and beautiful bridges. Can you see the river that runs through Paris? It's the Seine.

3

Tourists come from all over the world to see "The City of Light".
They go to Montmartre, the Champs-Élysées and visit the museums,
especially the Louvre. There you enter through a glass pyramid.
It's amazing! Inside, you can see statues and famous paintings.
Do you know the "Mona Lisa"?
I wonder what she is thinking about ...

NOTRE DAME DE PARIS

· LE LOUVRE ·

CADET DE

· BEAUBOURG ·

4

My favorite place is a park called Jardin du Luxembourg.
I often go there with my mom on Saturdays. We watch the
children sailing their boats on the pond. There are also ponies,
swings and a Guignol puppet theater. Do you know Guignol?
He's really funny!

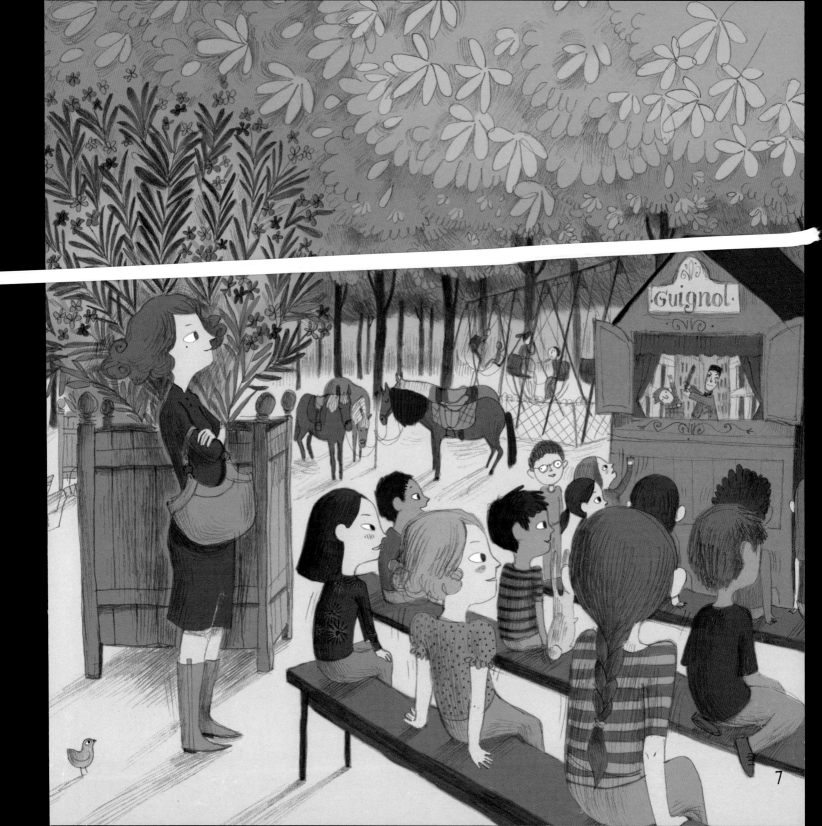

I live with my family in an apartment on the top floor under the roof. It is not very big, but it's very charming. It has funny windows. In France, we call them "sitting dogs" which amuses Tartine, my cat. Nicolas, my big brother, plays electric guitar. At the moment he is practicing with his friends for a big music festival called "Fête de la Musique". What a racket!

My parents leave early for work by "metro," or subway, or by
bus. Mom looks after babies in a nursery. Dad is the head chef
in a restaurant.
He is a very good cook, but Mom says he's a bit absent-minded.
It's true that he's got his head in the clouds.

I walk to school because it's just around the corner from our house. Every evening, I come home with my friends. There's a lady who helps us cross the street and then we go past the best bakery in the area. Look at the lovely cakes in the window! Sometimes we buy chocolate bread or other treats for a snack. Yum!

My friends and I are in the same class. We've known each other since preschool. Now we're at primary school and our teacher, Mrs. Dubois, is teaching us to read, write and count. I love reciting poetry. Today it's Lucie's turn to recite a poem in front of the class.

My favorite time is playtime. The boys play football and we play with elastics and skipping ropes. Sometimes the boys try to catch us. Manon calls this game "Catch-kiss." Paris is a very romantic city!

On Wednesdays, there is no school so we can do lots of activities!
My best friend, Manon, plays the piano and my friend Moussa plays
tennis. I do classical dance. One day, I would like to be a dancer at the
Paris Opera, but Mom says that you have to be a "little rat" first, so I'm
still thinking about it.

On the weekend, as soon as the weather is nice, we go in the car to our little house in the country. We have a pretty garden with flowers and a vegetable patch where I grow beautiful tomatoes and crunchy lettuce. My parents' friends often come and have lunch with us on Sundays. They say that my tomatoes are delicious!

20

When we spend the weekend in Paris, we often
go for a walk along the edge of the Seine River and
have an ice cream. I love rummaging around in the
booksellers' stalls and taking the "bateau-mouche"
to the Eiffel Tower. Do you know the Pont Neuf?
It's the oldest bridge in Paris!

23

On my birthday, I invited my friends to the house.
There were Lucie, Moussa, Manon, Fatima, Pierre and Li. Dad made us strawberry tarts and a huge chocolate cake. We listened to music and danced like madmen. It was a really great party!

25

For Christmas, we go to my grandparents' house in Saint-Rémy de Provence. We decorate the Christmas tree with my cousins and make a big nativity scene with very old figurines called "santons". My favorite one is the shepherd carrying a lamb on his shoulders. After we have eaten the Yule log, Grandma brings out the "thirteen desserts". What a feast! Then, we fall asleep in front of the fire while Grandpa reads us stories.

So there you are, the visit is over! I hope to see you soon in Paris. Goodbye!

28

Marie's Illustrated Vocabulary List

PAGES 2-3
Gourmet: The art of good cooking.

Department store: A large shop taking up several floors of a building, usually in the center of a town. It offers a large choice of goods organized into departments. The first department store in Paris, created in 1852, was the Bon Marché, which still exists today.

Museum: An establishment which presents a collection of works to its visitors, (statues, pictures...) or objects that have an artistic, scientific, historic or technical interest.

PAGES 6-7
Guignol: A puppet invented in Lyon, France in 1808, similar to Punch and Judy. It was turned into a children's show in Paris around 1850. The main characters are Guignol, his wife Madelon, Gnafron, Guignol's friend and his wife Toinon, the policeman, the judge and the owner.

PAGES 8-9
Sitting-dog window: A small window set into the slope of a roof whose shape from the side looks like a sitting dog.

PAGES 18-19
Little rat of the Opera: The name given to the children who study classical dance at the Paris Opera before becoming professional dancers. They are called "rat" because the sound of their slippers on the wooden floorboards sound like the patter of the rodents' feet.

PAGES 20-21

Vegetable patch: A small garden where plants and vegetables are grown for cooking.

PAGES 22-23

Second-hand bookseller: In Paris, there are almost 200 second-hand booksellers on the banks of the Seine. Their shops are big green boxes attached to the wall.

Bateau-mouche: A specially equipped boat with an open upper deck and seats that take tourists along the Seine River in Paris.

PAGES 26-27

Nativity scene: A small model of the stable where Jesus Christ was born, that Christians make for Christmas.

Yule Log: A cake in the shape of a log of wood which is traditionally eaten as part of the Christmas meal.

Santons: Small model figurines made from clay and used in the Nativity scene.

Thirteen Desserts: Traditionally from the South of France, the "thirteen desserts" represent Christ and the twelve Apostles. According to tradition, they must all be presented together on the table and each person eats a little of each one for good luck all year. Their composition varies from region to region, but often there are oranges, clementines or tangerines, nuts, dried figs, almonds, raisins, apples, pears, sweet pastries, pancakes, donuts, dates, preserved fruit, biscuits, and quince.

Your AV² Media Enhanced book gives you a fiction readalong online.
Log on to www.av2books.com and enter the unique book code from
page 2 to use your readalong.

AV² Readalong Navigation

HIGHLIGHTED TEXT

HOME

CLOSE

START READING

READ

TITLE INFORMATION

INFO

PAGE PREVIEW

PAGE TURNING

BACK NEXT

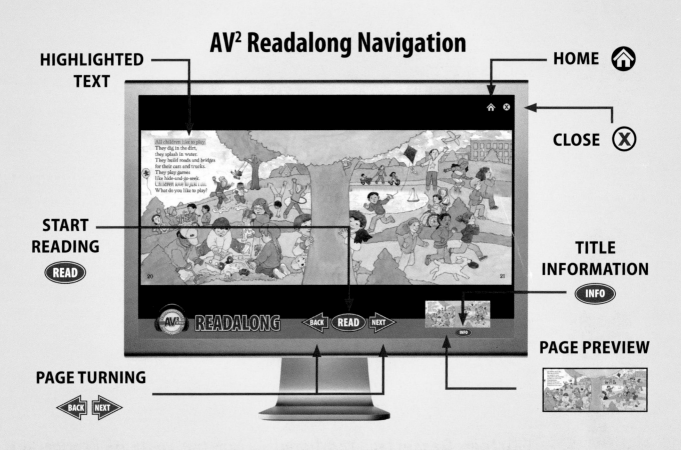

Published by AV² by Weigl
350 5th Avenue, 59th Floor New York, NY 10118
Websites: www.av2books.com   www.weigl.com

Copyright ©2015 AV² by Weigl

ABC MELODY Éditions
26, rue Liancourt 75014
Paris, France

Printed in the United States of America in North Mankato, Minnesota
1 2 3 4 5 6 7 8 9 0 18 17 16 15 14

042014
WEP080414

Library of Congress Control Number: 2014937141

ISBN 978-1-4896-2262-4 (hardcover)
ISBN 978-1-4896-2263-1 (single user eBook)
ISBN 978-1-4896-2264-8 (multi-user eBook)

Text copyright ©2009 by ABC MELODY.
Illustrations copyright ©2009 by ABC MELODY.
Published in 2009 by ABC MELODY.